Dear Parents:

Congratulations! Your child is taking the first steps on an exciting journey. The destination? Independent reading!

STEP INTO READING® will help your child get there. The program offers five steps to reading success. Each step includes fun stories and colorful art or photographs. In addition to original fiction and books with favorite characters, there are Step into Reading Non-Fiction Readers, Phonics Readers and Boxed Sets, Sticker Readers, and Comic Readers—a complete literacy program with something to interest every child.

Learning to Read, Step by Step!

Ready to Read   Preschool–Kindergarten
• big type and easy words • rhyme and rhythm • picture clues
For children who know the alphabet and are eager to begin reading.

Reading with Help   Preschool–Grade 1
• basic vocabulary • short sentences • simple stories
For children who recognize familiar words and sound out new words with help.

Reading on Your Own   Grades 1–3
• engaging characters • easy-to-follow plots • popular topics
For children who are ready to read on their own.

Reading Paragraphs   Grades 2–3
• challenging vocabulary • short paragraphs • exciting stories
For newly independent readers who read simple sentences with confidence.

Ready for Chapters   Grades 2–4
• chapters • longer paragraphs • full-color art
For children who want to take the plunge into chapter books but still like colorful pictures.

STEP INTO READING® is designed to give every child a successful reading experience. The grade levels are only guides; children will progress through the steps at their own speed, developing confidence in their reading.

Remember, a lifetime love of reading starts with a single step!

Step into Reading, Random House, and the Random House colophon are registered trademarks of Penguin Random House LLC.

Visit us on the Web!
StepIntoReading.com
rhcbooks.com

Educators and librarians, for a variety of teaching tools, visit us at RHTeachersLibrarians.com

ISBN 978-0-7364-4158-2 (trade) — ISBN 978-0-7364-9001-6 (lib. bdg.) —
ISBN 978-0-7364-4159-9 (ebook)

Printed in the United States of America

10 9 8 7 6 5 4 3 2 1

Disney
RAYA
AND
THE LAST DRAGON
TEACHING TUK TUK

by Mei Nakamura

illustrated by the Disney Storybook Art Team

Random House 🏠 New York

Raya is a young girl.

She lives with her father.

His name is Benja.

Raya and Benja

love to eat treats!

Benja has a surprise
for Raya.
He gives her a small box.

A new friend is inside!
His name is
Tuk Tuk.

Raya brings him outside.
She wants to teach
Tuk Tuk to be
a warrior.

But Tuk Tuk
wants to play!

Tuk Tuk chases a butterfly.

He falls on his back.

He takes a nap.

He does not train.

Raya does not know
how to teach Tuk Tuk.
She asks her father
what to do.

Benja gives
Raya some tea.
He tells her
to be patient.

Raya says she will try.
Raya and Benja are ready
for tea and treats.

Oh no!

The treats are gone!

Tuk Tuk ate the treats!

Raya has an idea.

She will teach

Tuk Tuk with treats!

Raya holds up a treat.

Tuk Tuk rolls to Raya!

She calls to Tuk Tuk.
Tuk Tuk follows!

Tuk Tuk crawls under a net.

He balances on sticks.

He rolls
down a board.

He gets plenty
of treats!

Day after day,
Raya and Tuk Tuk
train together.

They work hard.
They have treats
as a reward!

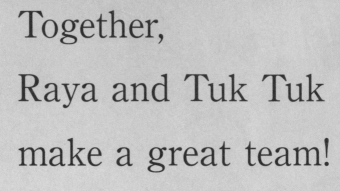

Together,
Raya and Tuk Tuk
make a great team!